A WILD BEAR CHASE

Someone was up here with him, and that someone was obviously after his bear.

The boot tracks stayed well to the side of the paw prints. Justin followed both sets through the snow halfway across the meadow and stopped. He put one foot down next to the boot track and then picked it up. The imprint was identical.

He was following his own tracks! The grizzly knew what Justin was doing and had outsmarted him. The bear had circled around and had cut back into the same trail.

She was hunting *him*.

GRIZZLY

A YEARLING BOOK

Published by
Bantam Doubleday Dell Books for Young Readers
a division of
Bantam Doubleday Dell Publishing Group, Inc.
1540 Broadway
New York, New York 10036

ISBN: 0-440-41217-X

Series design: Barbara Berger

Interior illustration by Michael David Biegel

Printed in the United States of America

November 1997

OPM   10   9   8   7   6   5   4   3   2   1

Dear Readers:

Real adventure is many things—it's danger and daring and sometimes even a struggle for life or death. From competing in the Iditarod dogsled race across Alaska to sailing the Pacific Ocean, I've experienced some of this adventure myself. I try to capture this spirit in my stories, and each time I sit down to write, that challenge is a bit of an adventure in itself.

You're all a part of this adventure as well. Over the years I've had the privilege of talking with many of you in schools, and this book is the result of hearing firsthand what you want to read about most—power-packed adventure and excitement.

You asked for it—so hang on tight while we jump into another thrilling story in my World of Adventure.

Gary Paulsen

GRIZZLY

CHAPTER 1

A low snarl filled the room. Justin McCallister's eyes flew open. He rolled out of bed. His feet barely touched the cold wooden floor planks as he ran to the window. "What is it, Radar? You hear something out there, girl?"

Justin crouched and put his hand on the young collie's neck. The dog was tense and the hair on her back was standing up. "Don't worry, girl. Old Molly is on duty tonight. She'll take care of any sorry coyotes that come around trying to bother the sheep."

Radar's ears went up. The growling changed to a high, piercing bark. She scratched wildly at the windowpane, then flipped around and tore out the bedroom door.

Justin was right behind her. He grabbed his uncle Mack's rifle from the rack above the living room fireplace, took a flashlight from the mantel, and yanked open the front door.

A bitter blast of cold Montana spring wind slammed into his body. It felt like a solid wall of ice and reminded him that he was barefoot and wearing only the lower half of his long johns.

Radar bounded into the darkness. Old Molly was barking now too, and Justin could hear the lambs in the south pen bleating. Shivering in the freezing wind, he pointed the light in the general direction of the noise.

"Can you see anything?"

Justin turned. His aunt Polly was standing in the doorway, holding out a down jacket.

"Not yet." Justin quickly slipped into the jacket and stepped off the porch.

"Be careful."

Justin nodded but didn't say anything. He levered a shell into the rifle.

A shrill yelp from one of the dogs cut the night. Justin stopped, fired one shot in the air, and started running.

When he reached the sheep he found the gate on the lamb pen ripped off its hinges and tossed aside. A mass of quivering animals were crushing each other in an effort to huddle in one corner of the pen.

Old Molly was on the ground near the opening. She was whimpering and blood was dripping from a long gash in her side.

Dead lambs were everywhere. Their bodies had been slashed and ripped to the bones. Great claw marks dug deep into their flanks.

Justin swallowed and pointed the light at the soft dirt. The tracks were plain: two large pads with five long scissorlike claws on each.

A grizzly.

Chapter 2

"Hold her, Justin. I need to get in at least three more good stitches."

Old Molly was stretched out on the kitchen table. She was weak from loss of blood. But that didn't stop her from trying to move every time Aunt Polly stuck the long needle and thread into her side to sew the ragged pieces of skin and fur together.

Justin tried to comfort the old dog as he put all his weight into holding her still. "It's for your own good, girl. A few days' rest and you'll be good as new."

4

"Wish I could say the same for that new crop of lambs." Uncle Mack sat near the table in his wheelchair, holding a clean bowl of hot water and some bandages.

Aunt Polly cut the thread and took a roll of bandages from her husband. "These things happen, Mack. It's part of ranching up here. You know that. We've been doing it almost thirty years."

"But grizzlies don't usually bother us. Whenever they did in the past it was because they were hungry. And then they only took a stray lamb or two. This is different. That bear was out for blood."

"You think it's the same one that hit Mr. Davis's place last week?" Justin asked.

"Gotta be." Uncle Mack looked thoughtful. "If I didn't have this broken hip, I'd go after it. Somebody's got to put a stop to the killing before all the ranchers up here are wiped out."

Radar sat up where she'd been lying by the door and started barking. Justin went to the window and moved the curtain. There were headlights approaching from down the road. "Someone's coming."

In a few moments there was a knock at the door. Justin opened it and a short man with a fringe of a white beard under his chin and a floppy felt hat on his head, stepped inside.

"Hello, Roy." Uncle Mack turned his chair to face the man. "What brings you out so early?"

The man saw Molly and removed his hat. "What happened?"

Uncle Mack sighed. "Justin thinks it was a grizzly, maybe even the one that was at your place a couple of days ago. We lost twelve head, and Old Molly got the stuffing beat out of her."

"That's why I'm here, Mack. I was hoping to warn you but I guess I'm too late. Luke Miller was hit last night too, right before you, it appears. He lost better than half his new crop of lambs."

Mack frowned. "Tell us how we can help."

"I've called a meeting of all the ranchers in a hundred-mile radius. There's no other way. That bear has to be stopped."

CHAPTER 3

"I'm glad you were safe in the shed when that grizzly came around last night." Justin playfully pulled the milk bottle out of the little lamb's greedy mouth. The fuzzy little creature dove for it and landed with both front hooves square in the middle of Justin's stomach.

"You are a pig," Justin laughed. "I should have named you Mr. Piggy instead of Blue."

"I think Blue is a good name." Aunt Polly came through the gate. "It suits him. He's got the look of a blue-ribbon champion. The only way you won't win first place at the county fair with him this fall is if the judges are stone blind.''

Justin proudly stroked the pushy little lamb. "You hear that, Blue? You're gonna be a winner!''

"You'd better get a move on, Justin. Mack's already in the truck. If we're going to be on time for the ranchers' meeting, we'd better get going.''

Justin stood up, gave the lamb one last pull on the bottle, then put it up on the shelf. "That's all for now, Blue. I'll be back later.''

Justin followed his aunt to the truck and waited for her to slide in beside Mack. Justin got behind the wheel and looked in the mirror to make sure Radar was safely in the back of the truck before he started the engine. Radar loved to go anywhere the truck was going.

Justin was only thirteen, too young for a license, but no one out here ever paid any attention to things like that. Practical things were what mattered on a ranch. Things like missing school during lambing season, driving to the store for a load of feed, and staying up in the high meadow in the summer for weeks at a time with the sheep.

As the old Ford rambled over the bumpy dirt roads, Justin glanced at his uncle. Mack McCallister was the only father he'd ever known. Justin's parents had died in a car wreck in Helena when he was a baby, and Mack and Polly had raised him.

Mack was well liked among the ranchers because he worked hard and was always the first to lend a neighbor a helping hand. That was how he'd broken his hip, trying to help some friends round up a stray bull. The bull had butted the horse Uncle Mack was riding, and he had been thrown. The doctors said the break in his hip was bad and would take several months to heal.

Justin slowed down, changed gears, and turned onto a gravel road. He ran a hand through his thick, dark brown hair.

"You look fine, son." Mack winked at him. "At least I'm pretty sure Sally Davis will think so."

"Cut it out." Justin's face flushed, the pink

traveling all the way to the tips of his ears. "We're here on business."

Mack raised an eyebrow. "I'll be sure and explain that to Sally."

Polly elbowed her husband as the truck came to a stop in front of a weather-beaten log house.

Justin hopped out and took the wheelchair from the back of the truck. "You stay there, Radar. This shouldn't take long."

He helped his uncle into the chair and pushed him up the path to the house. Mrs. Davis invited them in and offered them coffee.

Justin looked around the room. It was crowded with serious-looking ranchers and farmers worried about their livelihoods.

Roy Davis banged on the edge of a table with a butter knife. "Now that Mack's here we can get started." He waited for the room to quiet down. "As you all know, the reason I asked you to come was because of the killer grizzly."

Someone touched Justin's arm. "You want

coffee?" Sally Davis held a cup out and smiled.

Justin found himself staring at her, trying to figure out what was different. She still had the same blond hair and blue eyes, the same dimples. He'd grown up with her and they had always been best friends. But for some reason, things weren't the same lately, and he couldn't quite put his finger on why.

"Hel-looo? Anybody here want coffee?" Sally said teasingly.

Justin blinked and reached for the cup. "Uh . . . thanks." Embarrassed, he turned his attention back to Sally's father.

Mr. Davis was telling the group that he'd been in touch with the local forest rangers. "They say this bear fits the description of one from Yellowstone that lost two cubs to an illegal hunter. I tried to explain what's been going on up here, but they just don't seem to understand the problem."

"I don't think we ought to waste time talking." Luke Miller waved his fist in the air. "I think we should trap the thing and be done with it. All our ranches will be wiped out soon!"

"It's gotta be poisoned." A man in a long brown sheepskin coat stood up. "The only way to make sure it will leave us alone is to kill it."

"Maybe a group of us could go out after it," another man chimed in. "I'd like to go, of course, but we just finished lambing and I have to stay and tend to my stock."

"Unfortunately that's the boat most of us are in right now." Roy Davis rubbed his beard. "So I propose we send a representative to the head ranger's office in Billings and force them to take action. And I nominate Mack McCallister to be that representative."

CHAPTER 4

"I don't like leaving you," Aunt Polly said as she watched Justin put her bags and Uncle Mack's in the bed of the truck. "Especially with that crazy bear roaming around."

Mack leaned across the seat. "So far the grizzly hasn't come back to any place twice, but if he does, I don't want you taking any chances."

"You guys worry too much. It's not like you've never gone away before." Justin stepped back from the pickup. "Go on. And have a good time in Billings. I'll see you in a few days."

Aunt Polly put the truck in gear and started down the road. Justin waved and yelled, "Don't worry!"

When they were out of sight, he gave Radar a pat and headed for the pens. "We'll give everything one last check before we turn in."

He stopped by Blue's pen first. The lamb ran to the gate, sniffing for food. "It won't do you any good to beg. You've already had your supper. Now get back in the shed and go to sleep."

All evidence of the grizzly's attack the night before was gone. Justin had worked hard to clean things up and calm the sheep down.

Old Molly was nestled in a bed of straw in the barn. Justin dumped her water and gave her a clean bowl. "Here you go, girl. Just take it easy."

Justin closed the barn door and he and Radar trotted to the house. "Okay. It's just us guys. What should we do first?"

The collie barked and wagged her tail.

"Popcorn and a movie? Good choice." Justin opened the door and Radar ran past him into the kitchen.

Justin took a skillet out of the cabinet and put it on the stove. He poured in some oil and added the popcorn.

Radar's ears went up. She growled at the window.

"I'm hurrying. This stuff'll only cook so fast."

The collie barked and nervously ran to the window and back.

"What is it, girl? We were just out there. Everything's all right."

The dog snarled and jumped at the door.

"Okay, let's go take a look." Justin turned off the burner. "Hang on. I better get the rifle."

There was still enough light to see the outline of the pens from the porch. Justin squinted, trying to get a look at the sheep. Nothing seemed out of place, but Radar took off like a shot.

Before Justin could make it to the bottom

step he heard an enraged bellow and a crashing sound coming from the shed.

He ran to the barn, flattened himself against the wall, took a deep breath, and peered around the corner.

A huge bear had her head and one front shoulder through a hole she had punched in the shed wall and was angrily trying to get farther in.

She was the biggest animal Justin had ever laid eyes on. Her fur was tipped with silver and glistened, even in the dim light. The hump behind the bear's head told Justin she was a grizzly.

Radar ran up and bravely nipped at the bear's hind leg, darted back, then did it again. The grizzly was in no mood for games. She took a swipe at the dog with her front paw, catching Radar alongside the head.

It was like watching someone swat a fly. The collie sailed through the air, hit the barn wall, and fell to the ground, motionless.

The hole in the shed wall was bigger, and the bear was still trying to push inside.

Justin leveled his rifle. He took aim and pulled the trigger.

It was hard to tell in the fading light where the bullet hit. There was a dull thud, and the wounded bear arched sideways, pulling free of the hole. She stopped for a moment and looked at Justin, whose shaky hands were frantically trying to lever another round into the chamber of the rifle. Then the bear bolted into the woods.

Radar crawled weakly to her feet and barked at the shadows. Justin leaned the gun against the barn wall and knelt to examine the dog. As best he could tell, there were no broken bones. He stood and scolded the dog. "Next time, you better wait for me, girl. It's a miracle you aren't hurt."

Justin turned to the shed. The thick planked plywood wall was ruined. He'd have to patch it up for now and then try to rebuild it tomorrow.

He walked around to the front of the pen that was attached to the shed, and opened the gate. "Come on out, Blue. You're safe now. Blue?"

At the back of the pen near the shed door Justin saw a crumpled ball of white wool.

"No!" Justin ran to the lamb. Bright crimson blotches covered Blue's woolly side. Justin picked him up. But it was too late.

The lamb was dead.

CHAPTER 5

It was too dark to see the cold, angry puffs of air coming from Justin's nose and mouth. It was just barely morning. He'd already fed and watered the stock, making sure there was extra food and water in case he wasn't back in time for the night feeding.

He shrugged into his backpack and reached inside the gun cabinet for his uncle's favorite rifle. Justin had fired the gun once before. It had left a purple bruise above his armpit that hadn't gone away for a week.

He found a box of shells and loaded four

rounds into the rifle's magazine. The gun was powerful. He only hoped it would be power-ful enough.

"Let's go, Radar." Justin knew the grizzly was wounded. That would mean she couldn't travel as quickly as usual. It also meant she'd be meaner than ever.

Justin stepped off the porch and let Radar lead him through the pens to the edge of the woods. He unclipped a flashlight from his belt and scanned the ground. The grizzly's tracks were plainly visible, and so were sev-eral drops of dried blood.

The large paw prints were fairly easy to fol-low. The bear had crashed through the under-growth, leaving a wide path of broken tree limbs and crushed plants.

Radar sniffed the ground and trotted ahead. Justin held the rifle in both hands. Ready.

After a few hundred yards, the trail of blood stopped. Justin found a place where the bear had rolled over a large log and scratched all around it, probably looking for grubs. "I must not have hit her in a very good spot, girl. She doesn't seem to be hurting much, or in too big of a hurry."

A little while later the sun topped out over the blue-gray mountains and made tracking easier. Justin called Radar, who was eagerly trotting far ahead of him. "Don't get too far ahead, girl. Remember what happened the last time you got to the grizzly first."

The trail led up, toward taller timber. Justin crossed several steep gullies and climbed over two high ridges. Twice he lost sight of the tracks and had to let Radar choose their direction.

Justin followed the tracks all morning, but the grizzly didn't seem to be going anywhere in particular. Her trail twisted and took turns into snowy meadows and dense thickets that Justin could barely get through. Sometimes the trail took him up a ridge only to come back down the same side.

Finally he came to a small meadow where the bear's tracks were plain and plentiful. Justin frowned. There were other tracks there too. Human tracks.

Someone was up here with him, and that someone was obviously after his bear.

The boot tracks stayed well to the side of the paw prints. Justin followed both sets through the snow halfway across the meadow and stopped. He put one foot down next to the boot track and then picked it up. The imprint was identical.

He was following his own tracks! The grizzly knew what Justin was doing and had outsmarted him. She had circled around and had cut back into the same trail.

She was hunting *him.*

The hair went up on the back of his neck. He looked behind him, half expecting to see the grizzly running, coming for him.

The tables had been turned. A noise in the woods made him jump. He grabbed Radar's collar. A branch broke somewhere to his right, followed by the sound of crunching snow. The air smelled of wet, sour bear fur.

Radar was going crazy. It was all Justin could do to hold her. He watched the trees for any sign of movement. Everything was still.

Even the slight breeze that had been blowing had stopped.

Finally, his hand firmly on Radar's collar, Justin crept toward the woods.

At the edge of the trees he saw where the bear must have been standing on her hind legs, watching him. The tracks were there, but the grizzly was long gone. She'd played her trick and won, leaving Justin embarrassed, but alive.

CHAPTER 6

"This bear's a smart one." Justin clipped the chain to Radar's collar and sat down on a stack of wood behind the house. "I can't take you with me this time, Radar. You'll just get in the way. The only hope I have is to sneak up on her, and with you along she'll always know right where we are."

Radar whined and tugged at the chain.

"I know you want to come, but you can't. I called Sally. She'll be over later to check on things."

Justin winced as he remembered the story

he'd told Sally about having to go out and check on some stray sheep. He wouldn't have called her, but he was determined to get Blue's killer, even if it meant having to stay in the mountains for a couple of days.

He grabbed his bedroll and food pack and moved to the gate. The wind was worse today, whistling and howling through the trees. Justin set his jaw. It didn't matter how cold it became. Nothing would keep him from finding that bear.

The trail was old now, but it was all he had to go on. Uncle Mack had told him that bears usually followed a pattern when they traveled. If you searched and kept circling, sooner or later you would find fresh tracks.

Radar's barks of protest grew fainter as Justin strode quickly down the path. He'd decided not to follow the old tracks again. Instead he would cut through the forest to save time. The grizzly had headed for higher ground when he wounded her. With any luck, Justin would find her up there and catch her off guard.

On his way back home yesterday he'd had

time to think. The grizzly seemed to want to kill only for sport, not out of hunger. Maybe she was getting revenge against the hunters who had killed her cubs.

None of that mattered. The grizzly had come to the wrong ranch. Blue was dead, and Justin would settle for nothing less than the grizzly's life in return.

At midmorning he stopped on top of a high, thinly timbered ridge and took stock of his surroundings. Below him lay the upper valley of Moosehead Creek. The countryside was endless, a vast carpet of jagged green with a winding silver ribbon of water snaking its way along the bottom.

Justin had seen plenty of animal tracks. The forest was full of game. So far he had surprised a mountain goat, a black bear, and a few squirrels. But there was no sign of his grizzly.

Justin laid the rifle on the ground and took out his binoculars. He saw a thin wisp of smoke coming from somewhere in the next valley, probably from the camp of a ranch hand tending cattle or sheep, or perhaps from the camp of a backpacker.

He scanned the burn from an old fire that had taken place years ago, when he was a kid. It was still charred and dead-looking. Most of the trees had fallen to rot, but a few still stood watch like stately, burnt guardians.

A flock of white birds suddenly swept up into the air as if they had been startled. Justin kept his binoculars trained on the spot.

Something was moving around down there. Something big.

CHAPTER 7

 The mountains were beautiful to look at but difficult to travel through. What a person could see clearly in the distance might take several hours to reach on foot.

Justin found himself skirting washes and fallen trees, climbing up when he wanted to go down, cutting his way through dense brush and losing his bearings among the thick timbers. It was like being in a giant maze with no clear path to follow.

When he finally made it to the edge of the burn he took out his binoculars again. Something moved in the shadows. He focused on the spot. It was a bear, all right. He couldn't tell for certain if it was the grizzly, but it was big.

The burn was a dangerous place. In spots dead logs that had fallen on one another were stacked six feet deep, and the only way to cross them was to walk on top of the decayed wood.

The wind swept through the rotted trees, making them crack and sway. They could come crashing down at any second.

Justin adjusted his pack, shouldered the rifle, and started in. He was downwind from the bear, so he wasn't worried about the animal catching his scent.

The logs were unstable, and several times he smashed through the top layer and had to work to free his foot. Carefully he stepped on the next log and took out his binoculars. The bear was nowhere in sight. He'd taken so long to get to this point that the bear must have moved on.

He searched the trees. There was nothing. If the animal he'd seen was the grizzly, he'd been outsmarted once again. The bear was long gone and had left him standing in the middle of the treacherous burn.

Justin let the binoculars hang from his neck and studied his situation. He decided the best thing to do was head for the spot where he'd last seen the bear and look for tracks.

He stepped up on another pile of logs, but before he could bring his other leg up, the pile shifted. The top log rolled out from under him and he pitched backward.

He fell hard. Logs careened over him, slamming into his head and shoulders and crushing him under their weight.

CHAPTER 8

 Justin opened his eyes. Dirt and wood rot stung them. He tried to move his hand to brush the debris away but his arms were jammed tight against his sides.

He was flat on his back looking up at the tangle of charred dead trees that had him trapped. Tiny dots of light shone through cracks above. His legs were twisted at strange angles, but there was no pain, just the crushing pressure of the timber on top of him.

His body fought against the weight, but it was useless. He was buried alive. He closed his eyes again and thought of Mack and Polly. They would eventually come looking for him, but they'd never be able to find him under the burn. Would he ever see them again?

Suddenly he heard the footsteps of someone walking through the burn toward him.

"Help," Justin said weakly, coughing. "I'm here, under the trees."

He listened and hoped. The footsteps were steadily getting closer, crunching slowly on the decayed debris.

He had been found. Someone had seen the accident and was coming to help. Above him, Justin could hear the sound of heavy logs being moved away one by one.

Then there was something else. A low guttural noise followed by heavy breathing and an impatient, whooshing snort.

Justin froze in terror. He had no idea where the rifle had fallen. He forced himself to think. Old-timers claimed bears wouldn't bother you if you didn't try to get away and made no sudden movements. He decided to play dead.

The pressure was off his legs now. Through his nearly closed eyelids Justin could see the bear heaving timbers out of her way as if they were matchsticks. It was the grizzly. The grizzly that had killed Blue.

Justin's heart raced. The bear was enormous. Her fur was brown with shining silver tips. And her paws—her paws were long and hairy, with curved ivory claws that looked like knives.

Justin squeezed his eyes shut. He felt a tug on his leg. *This is it,* he thought. *She's going to tear me apart and eat me piece by piece.*

The grizzly viciously yanked him out of the entanglement and dragged him by one boot across the burn.

The bear was lighter on her feet than Justin could ever have imagined, but still they both fell through the dead wood in places, and several times the bear had to let go of him to pull herself out of a hole.

Justin fought the urge to resist, to stand up and run. He had no choice but to continue to play dead. His head bumped into everything they crossed, and his body was scraped and bleeding. His left arm started to throb as if it was broken.

When they were finally out of the burn the grizzly continued to drag him by the leg as if he weighed no more than a child's rag doll. She pulled him up a bluff to a rock ledge, tossed him underneath it, and then started scratching the ground, covering him with leaves and dirt. She didn't stop until Justin was covered from head to toe.

Justin's whole body ached, and the throbbing in his arm was getting worse. He longed to reach up and move the leaves off his face, but he knew he could not move. He had to wait.

The bear stepped around him, looking at her handiwork. Then she snorted, whirled, and loped off.

Justin swallowed and wondered why the bear hadn't shredded him on the spot the way she had the sheep. He let out a deep breath and tried to catch another. Probably she had already eaten and was saving him for her evening meal.

He carefully raised his head a few inches. The leaves fell to the side, allowing him to breathe more easily and see where he was.

The grizzly had brought him to an overhang above the burn. Below, Justin could see the charred forest and the river. The bear was nowhere in sight.

Justin moved slowly, hoping he wouldn't attract any attention in case the bear was waiting out there somewhere, watching. He crawled to his feet and took a shaky step. His left arm dangled uselessly by his side and every part of him hurt, but there was no time to think about it. He forced himself to move, to leave, to survive.

Climbing the hill was out of the question right now. He'd have to head for the river.

CHAPTER 9

The cold, clear water tasted good. Justin wished he could lie on the muddy bank forever, just drinking and resting.

But there was the grizzly. She would soon discover he was gone and come looking for him. He had to fight the pain and keep going, crawling if necessary, until he was home.

He still had his backpack, but his rifle was gone and his binoculars were in pieces. He was completely defenseless against the bear.

Slowly Justin inched to his feet and waded into the river, hoping his scent would be lost in the water and the bear would be unable to follow him. His plan was to cut a wide circle around her territory and—he hoped—make it safely back to the ranch.

He sloshed through the freezing water and crawled several hundred yards downstream. The wind was merciless, whipping at his cold wet pants legs and boots.

Resting on the bank, Justin checked his pack. The bottom of the pack had been ripped and his bedroll was missing. Most of the contents were probably scattered across the burn. In the zippered front pouch he found a small box of matches and stuffed them into his coat pocket.

The sun was going down, and he was cold, tired, and hungry. He had never been this far into the mountains. He walked on, keeping up a slow but steady pace until the light was almost gone.

At dusk, he found a sheltered hollow. Using his good arm, he scraped up some pine needles and gathered a few sticks of dry wood for a fire.

Once he had a small blaze going, he sat

down to examine his wounds. He tried to take his coat off but found that the sleeve was glued to his bad arm with dried blood. He decided to leave it alone for the moment so that it wouldn't start bleeding again.

Lying down on the hard ground as close to the fire as he dared, Justin tried to go to sleep. His arm continued to throb, and it was hours before he finally dozed off.

It seemed as if he had been asleep only a few minutes when he heard something crashing through the brush near him.

Justin sat up and whirled around. He found himself face to face with the grizzly. She stood on her hind legs a few feet from him, growling and sniffing.

Justin scrambled to the other side of the fire, crouched low behind the blaze, and waited.

The bear moved closer and snorted. She swayed back and forth, her eyes glowing red in the reflection of the flames, as if she was trying to make up her mind whether or not to charge through the fire at him.

Justin held his breath, waiting, knowing he might die now, that he couldn't do anything to stop her. But suddenly the great beast dropped to all fours, turned, and padded noiselessly back into the shadows.

CHAPTER 10

Justin could hear the beating of his heart. The grizzly was still out there, waiting. At any moment she could change her mind and come back for him. He had to have a plan.

In the cold pink light of morning Justin looked at the trees around him. If he could get to one and climb it, the bear wouldn't be able to catch him. He had read somewhere that cubs would climb trees but that adult bears couldn't.

He studied the tree closest to him. It was

tall, with no branches near the bottom that he could grab. Silently he moved away from the fire and back toward the river. There were younger trees along the river. All he had to do was find the right one.

There was a noise in the trees to his right. Out of the corner of his eye he saw a patch of silver fur keeping pace with him as he moved. He wanted to run, to take his chances, but he held himself in check.

He was nearly out of the timber when he saw it. Lodged in the branches of a tall spruce was a tree that had been knocked over by the wind. It made a perfect ladder to the higher branches of the spruce.

The grizzly was visible now. Justin put his hand on the windfall, took a deep breath, and scrambled up the tree as fast as he could using just one arm.

The bear charged out of the trees, bellowing like an angry bull. She made a swipe at him and caught the heel of his boot with one of her claws, almost knocking him out of the tree.

He hung on and kept climbing until he was high above the grizzly's head and out of reach of her deadly paws.

The bear dropped onto all fours and circled the tree. Then she moved back a few feet and sat on her haunches to wait.

CHAPTER 11

 A blast of cold wind hit him in the face. Justin jerked awake. He had fallen asleep with his head resting against the big spruce.

He looked below. The grizzly was still there, a few yards away from the tree, tearing at a stump. She was completely absorbed in her project, hunting for food.

Justin started to inch down to the branch below him. The instant he moved, the grizzly sat up and scrambled under the tree.

She had no intention of letting him get

away this time. Her large head swayed back and forth as she sniffed the air.

"Go on!" Justin yelled. "Get out of here and leave me alone."

The grizzly cocked her head to one side as if the sound of Justin's voice intrigued her. After a few moments she left the tree and headed for the river. She turned back once to look at him, and then went on.

Justin considered climbing down, but he realized the bear could outrun him and he didn't want to be caught on the ground.

At the river, the grizzly ambled lazily into the flowing water, stuck her paw in, and scooped water and a cutthroat trout up onto the bank. Justin was amazed at her quickness. Almost before he could blink, she did it again, popping the second wriggling fish up onto the bank before scrambling ashore to eat both fish.

Justin was envious. He'd been so angry, and in such a hurry, he hadn't eaten since the grizzly had murdered Blue. He shifted his aching arm, stretched his legs, and tried not to think about the emptiness in his stomach.

The grizzly stood up to see what he was doing. She shot him an angry warning snort. Then she crossed the river and started up the mountain on the other side.

Justin hugged the tree with his good arm, watching her go. He couldn't believe his good luck. The grizzly must have become tired of toying with him.

He waited until she was no longer visible and then cautiously climbed down from his perch. To be on the safe side, he waited by the tree to see if she was playing a trick to lure him down.

She didn't come back.

As fast as he could move, Justin headed in the opposite direction. He didn't care where he was going as long as it was away from the grizzly.

CHAPTER 12

 He was hopelessly lost. Justin put his hand up to shield his eyes from the sun. Every tree he passed looked the same as a thousand others.

His stomach yearned for food, and his arm hurt all the time now, making it hard to think about anything except the pain. But he had to keep moving. At least that was the way he figured it. If the bear came looking for him again, he wanted to be far away.

A twig snapped. Justin jumped and looked around. It was only a deer running for cover.

When he had panicked and run earlier, he

had moved away from the river. Now he was wishing he had stayed with it. He could almost taste the cool water, and with any luck he might have been able to snag a trout. Instead he was in the middle of a wilderness with nothing to drink or eat.

He studied the angle of the sun and made a guess at the location of the river.

He walked for a couple of hours. A strange humming sound was coming from somewhere to the east. The closer he moved to the noise, the louder it became, until it was almost a roar.

Pulling back some branches, Justin suddenly saw before him a magnificent waterfall. It tumbled over the edge of a thirty-foot drop. He ran to the river's edge and scooped sloppy handfuls of water into his dry mouth.

He wiped his face with the sleeve of his coat and stepped back. He recalled seeing a waterfall on a map of this area. If he remembered correctly, there were hiking trails and a ranger station near here.

Hope welled up inside him. If he could find one of those trails . . .

He heard a growl behind him. He turned in time to see the grizzly charge. She came thundering out of the trees straight at him.

There was nowhere to hide. He backed into the water. The bear didn't slow down. She hit him full force, knocking him onto his back in the river.

She reached for him, but the river was faster. The current jerked him out to the center and shoved him under, pulling him toward the waterfall.

The grizzly went in after him. The water slammed into her, knocking her off balance. She struggled, but the swift water was too strong.

CHAPTER 13

Justin felt as if he had been run over by a train. His head was pounding. He raised himself on his elbows and discovered he was still in the water. But the waterfall was above him now.

He remembered going over. It was like a bad dream. He'd had the sensation of flying—until he'd hit bottom.

A sour smell came to his nostrils, the smell of grizzly. He sat up, his eyes darting all around. There she was, lying on her back halfway out of the water.

Justin stood up to run. But the bear didn't move. Her eyes were closed, and blood trickled from the corner of her mouth.

He should have been glad that at last the great bear was dead. But he wasn't. This was the killer that had murdered Blue and the other sheep. This grizzly had put Mr. Miller out of business and had tried more than once to kill Justin too.

But Justin couldn't bring himself to be happy. The bear had been smart. And if it hadn't been for her pulling him out, he'd probably still be trapped under the burn.

Justin waded to shore and gave the great bear one last look. Then he started walking. A few yards from the riverbank he spotted a well-used hiking trail.

His steps grew faster. The sun was going down. He wasn't going to spend another night in the mountains if he could help it.

Walking was easier now. The path curved downhill. Justin rounded a corner and almost ran smack into a tall, dark-haired forest ranger dressed in a green uniform.

"Hold on, son. What's the . . . hey, you look awful! Are you hurt?"

Justin managed a thin smile. "I think my arm's broken. Boy, am I glad to see you."

"Here. Sit on this log and let me take a look." The ranger took his knife and slit the sleeve of Justin's coat. "What are you doing up here? Hiking?"

"It's a long story. I live on the McCallister ranch on the other side of Moosehead. My name's Justin McCallister."

"I know a McCallister. Mack McCallister."

"He's my uncle."

"You're a long way from home, son. What on earth are you doing way over here?"

Justin looked at the ground. "I went after a bear. A grizzly. She broke into our place and killed my pet lamb."

The ranger ran his fingers expertly down Justin's arm. "It's broken, all right." He stood. "I'm going to pretend I didn't hear what you just told me. Considering I'd have to lock you up if I *had* heard it."

"Oh, I didn't kill her. She's dead, though.

We tangled at the waterfall. She fell over and must have hit her head on a rock or something. Anyway, she's lying on the bank if you want to go look."

The ranger sighed. "I guess I'd better. Can you hang on here for a few minutes?"

Justin nodded. "As long as you promise to come back."

The ranger smiled. "Promise." He turned and trotted up the trail.

Justin held his aching arm. He'd learned a lot in the past two days, not just about bears but also about himself.

He'd been so sure of himself before, and so angry. He sighed. Uncle Mack probably wouldn't be too happy with him, and Aunt Polly . . . well, he'd be grounded for at least ten years.

The ranger took longer than Justin thought he should. Justin stood and was about to go looking when he heard footsteps coming down the trail.

The ranger loped into sight. "Sorry I took so long. I wasn't sure exactly where to look."

"That's okay. Are you going to have some-one come up and bury her?"

"I hate to break this to you, son, but there's nothing up there to bury. I searched both sides of the river and finally found her tracks heading off into the woods. That grizzly's as alive as you and me."

Justin sat back on the log and sighed.

The ranger misunderstood. "Don't let it worry you. We'll have a team up here tomor-row to look into this. If that bear is a problem, we'll take care of it."

"I wasn't worried. This may sound kind of funny, but I'm glad she didn't die."

The ranger shrugged as he rigged a sling for Justin's arm with his belt. He helped Justin to his feet. "Come on, son. Let's get you home."

"Believe me, I'm ready."

GARY PAULSEN
ADVENTURE GUIDE

GRIZZLY BEARS

The Bear Essentials—Facts About Grizzly Bears

- Grizzlies are found in the western United States and northern Canada.
- Grizzlies are endangered in many areas.
- Adult grizzly bears are usually six to eight feet tall from tip of nose to tail and can weigh between four hundred and a thousand pounds.
- The grizzly's life span is fifteen to twenty-five years.
- Grizzlies are omnivorous (they eat both meat and plants), but about eighty-five percent of their diet is plant material. They eat twenty-five to thirty-five pounds of food a day!
- You can tell the difference between a black bear and a grizzly bear by the hump of muscle between the grizzly's shoulders. Also, a grizzly's claws are longer and its toes are straighter and closer together than a black bear's.
- If a human baby grew at the same rate as a grizzly cub, the baby would weigh six thousand pounds by the time it became an adult.
- One of the greatest dangers for grizzly cubs is adult grizzly bears, which sometimes catch and eat the cubs.

Grizzly Survival Tips—Hiking and Camping in Grizzly Bear Country

- Respect all bears. Never approach or feed a bear.
- Be aware. Bears can run as fast as horses—uphill or downhill.
- If you're camping or hiking in an area where grizzly bears might live, be alert. Make noise as you hike by singing or occasionally calling out. You don't want to surprise a grizzly!
- Bears are attracted to the smell of food. When camping, don't sleep in the same clothes you cook food in. Store food so that bears can't smell or reach it, and never keep *any* food in your tent.

Don't miss all the exciting action!

**Read the other action-packed books in
Gary Paulsen's
WORLD OF ADVENTURE!**

The Legend of Red Horse Cavern

Will Little Bear Tucker and his friend Sarah Thompson have heard the eerie Apache legend many times. Will's grandfather especially loves to tell them about Red Horse—an Indian brave who betrayed his people, was beheaded, and now haunts the Sacramento Mountain range, searching for his head. To Will and Sarah it's just a story—until they decide to explore a new-found mountain cave, a cave filled with dangerous treasures.

Deep underground, Will and Sarah uncover an old chest stuffed with a million dollars. But now armed bandits are after them. When they find a gold Apache statue hidden in a skull, it seems Red Horse is hunting them, too. Then they lose their way, and each step they take in the damp, dark cavern could be their last.

Rodomonte's Revenge

Friends Brett Wilder and Tom Houston are video game whizzes. So when a new virtual reality arcade called Rodomonte's Revenge opens near their home, they make sure they're its first customers. The game is awesome. There are flaming fire rivers to jump, beastly buzz-bugs to fight, and ugly tunnel spiders to escape. If they're good enough they'll face Rodomonte, an evil giant waiting to do battle within his hidden castle.

But soon after they play the game, strange things start happening to Brett and Tom. The computer is taking over their minds. Now everything that happens in the game is happening in real life. A buzz-bug could gnaw off their ears. Rodomonte could smash them to bits. Brett and Tom have no choice but to play Rodomonte's Revenge again. This time they'll be playing for their lives.

Escape from Fire Mountain

". . . please, anybody . . . fire . . . need help."

That's the urgent cry thirteen-year-old Nikki Roberts hears over the CB radio the weekend she's left alone in her family's hunting lodge. The message also says that the sender is trapped near a bend in the river. Nikki knows it's dangerous, but she has to try to help. She paddles her canoe downriver, coming closer to the thick black smoke of the forest fire with each stroke. When she reaches the bend, Nikki climbs onshore. There, covered with soot and huddled on a rock ledge, sit two small children.

Nikki struggles to get the children to safety. Flames roar around them. Trees splinter to the ground. But as Nikki tries to escape the fire, she doesn't know that two poachers are also hot on her trail. They fear that she and the children have seen too much of their illegal operation—and they'll do anything to keep the kids from making it back to the lodge alive.

The Rock Jockeys

Devil's Wall.

Rick Williams and his friends J.D. and Spud—the Rock Jockeys—are attempting to become the first and youngest climbers to ascend the north face of their area's most treacherous mountain. They're also out to discover if a B-17 bomber rumored to have crashed into the mountain years ago is really there.

As the Rock Jockeys explore Devil's Wall, they stumble upon the plane's battered shell. Inside, they find items that seem to have belonged to the crew, including a diary written by the navigator. Spud later falls into a deep hole and finds something even more frightening: a human skull and bones. To find out where they might have come from, the boys read the navigator's story in the diary. It reveals a gruesome secret that heightens the dangers the mountain might hold for the Rock Jockeys.

Hook 'Em, Snotty!

Bobbie Walker loves working on her grandfather's ranch. She hates the fact that her cousin Alex is coming up from Los Angeles to visit and will probably ruin her summer. Alex can barely ride a horse and doesn't know the first thing about roping. There is no way Alex can survive a ride into the flats to round up wild cattle. But Bobbie is going to have to let her tag along anyway.

Out in the flats the weather turns bad. Even worse, Bobbie knows that she'll have to watch out for the Bledsoe boys, two mischievous brothers who are usually up to no good. When the boys rustle the girls' cattle, Bobbie and Alex team up to teach the Bledsoes a lesson. But with the wild bull Diablo on the loose, the fun and games may soon turn deadly serious.

Danger on Midnight River

Daniel Martin doesn't want to go to Camp Eagle Nest. He wants to spend the summer as he always does: with his uncle Smitty in the Rocky Mountains. Daniel is a slow learner, but most other kids call him retarded. Daniel knows that at camp, things are only going to get worse. His nightmare comes true when he and three bullies must ride the camp van together.

On the trip to camp, Daniel is the butt of the

bullies' jokes. He ignores them and concentrates on the roads outside. He thinks they may be lost. As the van crosses a wooden bridge, the planks suddenly give way. The van plunges into the raging river below. Daniel struggles to shore, but the driver and the other boys are nowhere to be found. It's freezing, and night is setting in. Daniel faces a difficult decision. He could save himself . . . or risk everything to try to rescue the others, too.

The Gorgon Slayer

Eleven-year-old Warren Trumbull has a strange job. He works for Prince Charming's Damsel in Distress Rescue Agency, saving people from hideous monsters, evil warlocks, and wicked witches. Then one day Warren gets the most dangerous assignment of all: He must exterminate a Gorgon.

Gorgons are horrible creatures. They have green scales, clawed fingers, and snakes for hair. They also have the power to turn people to stone. Warren doesn't want to be a stone statue for the rest of his life. He'll need all his courage and skill—and his secret plan—to become a true Gorgon slayer.

The Gorgon howls as Warren enters the dark basement to do battle. Warren lowers his eyes, raises his sword and shield, and leaps into action. But will his plan work?

Captive!

Roman Sanchez is trying hard to deal with the death of his dad—a SWAT team member gunned down in the line of duty. But Roman's nightmare is just beginning.

When masked gunmen storm into his classroom, Roman and three other boys are taken hostage. They are thrown into the back of a truck and hauled to a run-down mountain cabin, miles from anywhere. They are bound with rope and given no food. With each passing hour the kidnappers' deadly threats become even more real.

Roman knows time is running out. Now he must somehow put his dad's death behind him so that he and the others can launch a last desperate fight for freedom.

The Treasure of El Patrón

Tag Jones and his friend Cowboy spend their days diving in the azure water surrounding Bermuda. It's not just for fun—Tag knows that somewhere in the coral reef there's a sunken ship full of treasure. His father died in a diving accident looking for the ship, and Tag won't give up until he finds it.

Then the ship's manifest of the Spanish galleon *El Patrón* turns up, and Tag can barely contain his excitement. *El Patrón* sank in 1614, carrying "unknown cargo." Tag knows that *this* is the ship his father was looking for. And he's not the least bit scared off by the rumors that *El Patrón* is cursed. But when two tourists want Tag to retrieve some mysterious sunken parcels for them, Tag and Cowboy may be in dangerous water, way over their heads!

Skydive!

Jesse Rodriguez has a pretty exciting job for a thirteen-year-old, working at a small flight and skydiving school near Seattle. Buck Sellman, the owner of the school, lets Jesse help out around the airport and is teaching him all about skydiving. Jesse can't wait until he's sixteen and old enough to make his first jump.

Then Robin Waterford walks in with her father one day to sign up for lessons, and strange things start to happen. Photographs that Robin takes of the airfield mysteriously disappear from her locker. And Robin and Jesse discover that someone at the airfield is involved in an illegal transportation operation. Jesse and Robin soon find themselves in the middle of real danger and are forced to make their first skydives very unexpectedly—using only one parachute!

The Seventh Crystal

Chosen One,
The ancient palace lies in the Valley of Zon.
It is imperative that you come immediately.
You are my last hope. Look for the secret path.
The stars will lead the way. Take care. The eyes
of Mogg are everywhere.

As if school bullies weren't enough of a problem, now Chris Masters has a computer game pushing him around! Ever since The Seventh Crystal arrived anonymously in the mail one day, Chris has been obsessed with it—it's the most challenging game he's ever played. But when the game starts to take over, Chris is forced to face a lean, mean, *medieval* bully.

The Creature of Black Water Lake

Thirteen-year-old Ryan Swanner and his mom just moved to the mountain resort of Black Water Lake. The locals say that beneath the lake's seemingly calm surface, a giant, ancient creature lives. But Ryan's new friend Rita tells him that's just hogwash. She's not afraid to go fishing out on the lake, even though, oddly, the lake seems to be nearly empty of fish. One day Ryan sees a small animal fall from a tree into the lake—and never surface again. Something *is* in the lake. And it's alive. . . .

Time Benders

Superbrain Zack Griffin and hoops fanatic Jeff Brown wouldn't normally hang together. But when both boys win trips to a famous science laboratory, they find out they have one thing in common: a serious case of curiosity. And when they sneak into the lab to check out the time-bending machine again, they end up in Egypt—in 1350 B.C.!